My Cat Just Sleeps

Joanne Partis

OXFORD
UNIVERSITY PRESS

My friends have all got fun cats.

They jump,

and chase,

and play

and hunt.

But my cat doesn't do any of those things.

My cat just sleeps.

George's cat climbs trees.
He can climb right up to the
highest branches and he
never, ever, falls.

But my cat won't even climb a small tree.

My cat just sleeps.

Harry's cat digs up worms
in the garden.

She likes carrying them around in her mouth.

But my cat isn't interested in worms.

My cat just sleeps.

Molly's cat plays with the fish in her pond. She splashes with her paws, while she licks her lips.

But my cat doesn't like fishing.

My cat just sleeps.

I wish my cat was exciting.
But all he does
is snooze ...

and yawn ...

and purr.

He cuddles up
on my lap,

and he keeps my feet
warm at night.

My cat does LOTS of things!

I love my cat.

Purr
Purr
Purr

But I wish I knew why he is always so sleepy.